MOO MOO

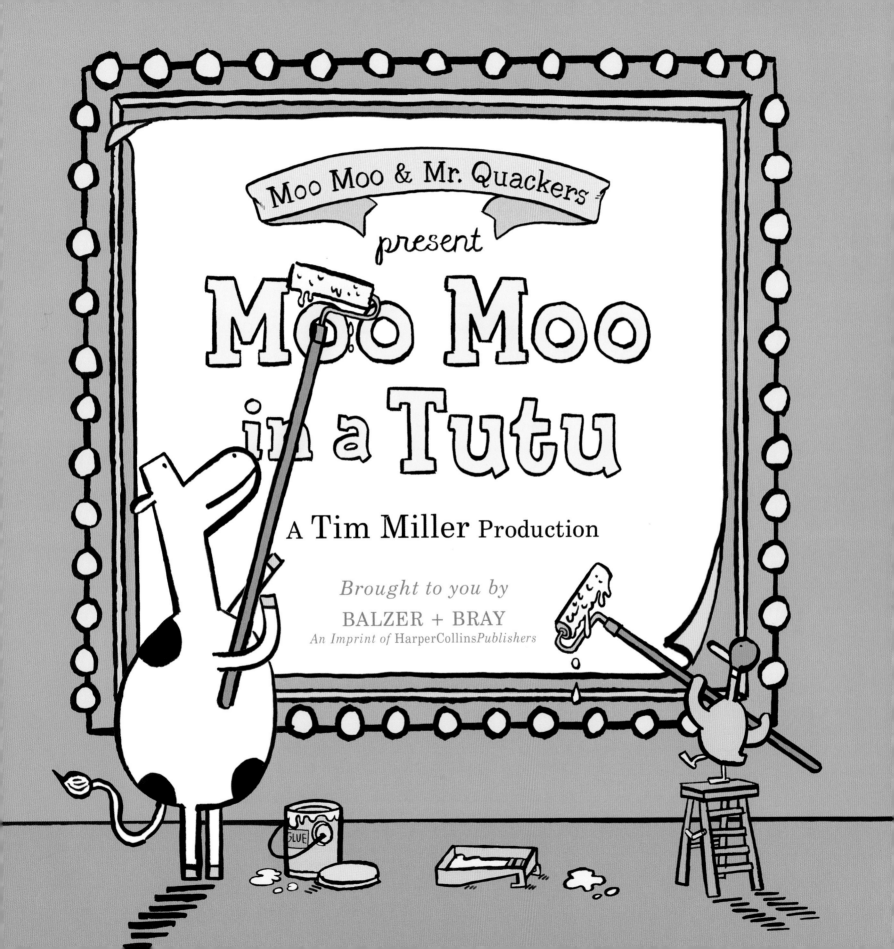

Balzer + Bray is an imprint of HarperCollins Publishers.

Moo Moo & Mr. Quackers Present: Moo Moo in a Tutu
Copyright © 2017 by Tim Miller

Library of Congress Control Number: 2015958373
ISBN 978-0-06-241440-3

The pictures in this book were made with brush and ink and digital hocus-pocus.
Typography by Dana Fritts
16 17 18 19 20 SCP 10 9 8 7 6 5 4 3 2 1
❖
First Edition

For Nancy

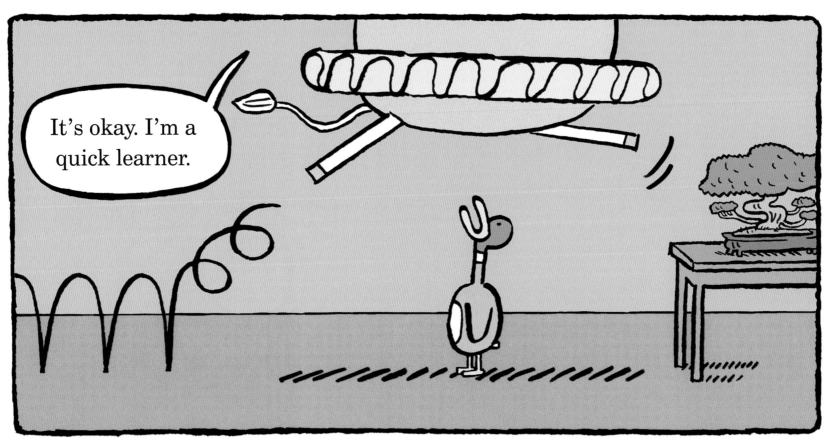

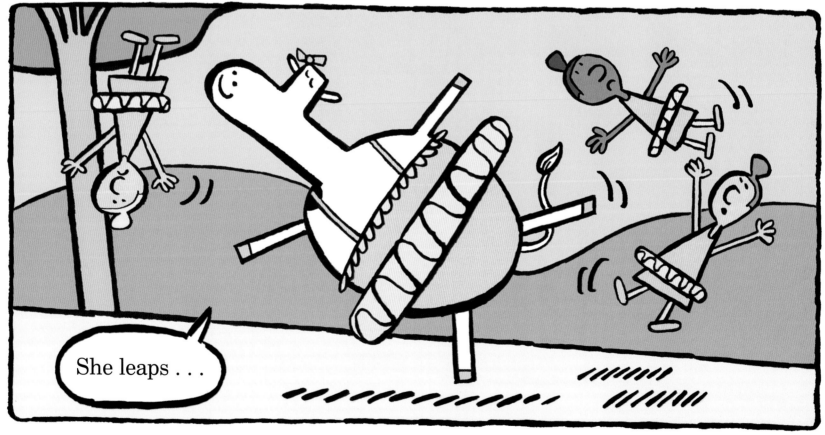

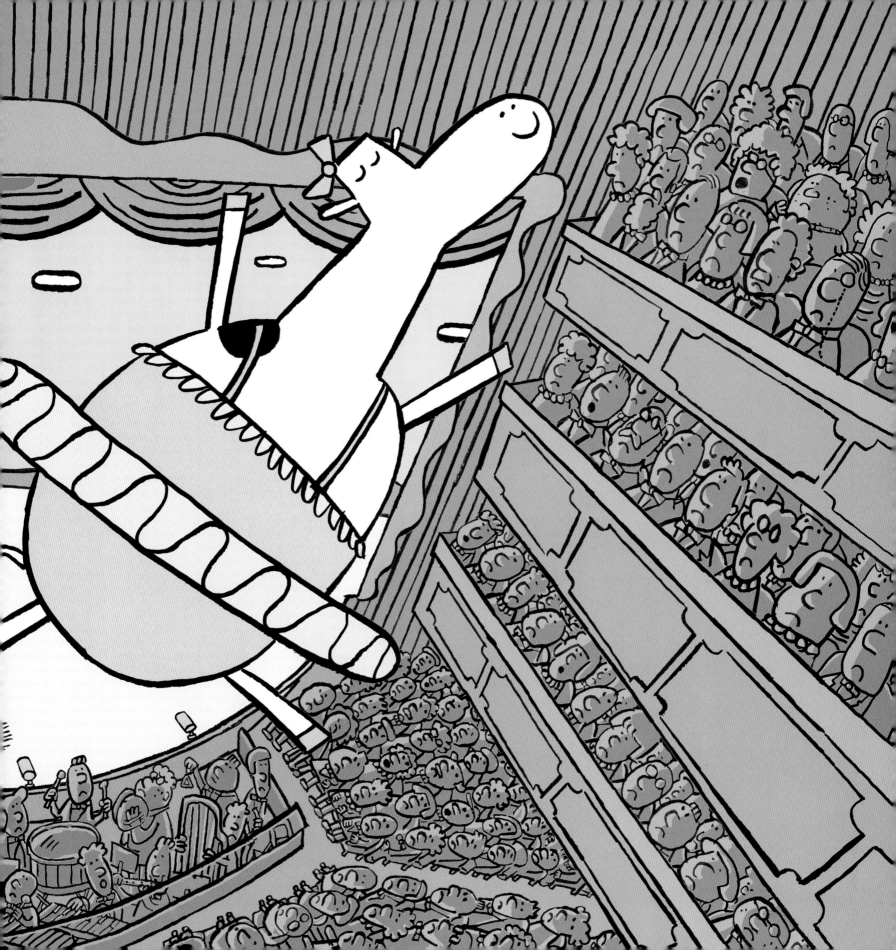